# A Note to Parents

**Read to your child...**

★ Reading aloud is one of the best ways to develop your child's love of reading. Read together at least 20 minutes each day.

★ Laughter is contagious! Read with feeling. Show your child that reading is fun.

★ Take time to answer questions your child may have about the story. Linger over pages that interest your child.

**...and your child will read to you.**

★ Follow cues from your child to know when he wants to join in the reading.

★ Support your young reader. Give him a word whenever he asks for it.

★ Praise your child as he progresses. Your encouraging words will build his confidence.

**You can help your Level 1 reader.**

★ Reading begins with knowing how a book works. Show your child the title and where the story begins.

★ Ask your child to find picture clues on each page. Talk about what is happening in the story.

★ Point to the words as you read so your child can make the connection between the print and the story.

★ Ask your child to point to words she

★ Let your child supply the rhyming w

D1055809

***Most of all, enjoy your reading time***

**—Bernice Cullinan, Ph.D.,**
**Professor of Reading, New York University**

Fisher-Price and related trademarks and copyrights are used under
license from Fisher-Price, Inc., a subsidiary of Mattel, Inc.,
East Aurora, NY 14052 U.S.A.
©2003, 2000 Mattel, Inc.
All Rights Reserved. **MADE IN CHINA**.
Published by Reader's Digest Children's Books
Reader's Digest Road, Pleasantville, NY U.S.A. 10570-7000
Copyright © 2000 Reader's Digest Children's Publishing, Inc.
All rights reserved. Reader's Digest Children's Books is a trademark
and Reader's Digest and All-Star Readers are registered trademarks of
The Reader's Digest Association, Inc.
Conforms to ASTM F963 and EN 71
10 9

*Library of Congress Cataloging-in-Publication Data*

Gabriel, Nat.
A day with May / by Nat Gabriel ; illustrated by Jerry Smath.
p. cm. — (All-star readers. Level 1)
Summary: A brother and sister play indoors and outdoors on a rainy day.
ISBN 1-57584-384-6 (alk. paper)
[1. Rain and rainfall Fiction. 2. Brothers and sisters Fiction.
3. Stories in rhyme.] I. Smath, Jerry, ill. II. Title. III. Series.
PZ8.3.G98954Day 2000 [E]—dc21 99-34717

# A Day with May

by Nat Gabriel
illustrated by Jerry Smath

All-Star Readers®

Reader's Digest Children's Books™
Pleasantville, New York • Montréal, Québec

Dad is busy.

I help watch May.

It's raining outside.

It's an inside day.

May makes a party
for the cat.

A B
J K

Then, she plays dress-up.

She makes me wear a hat.

I make a tent.

May makes a mess.

Dad says, "Shall we take her out?"

I say, "Yes!"

May jumps in a puddle.
"Watch out, Dad!"

May's all muddy.
May feels glad!

May comes in,
but she's upset.

She wants to stay out.
She wants to stay wet!

I have a plan.
Dad says, "Okay!"

May is happy.
I saved the day!

May is done.
She's nice and dry.

Then May needs a nap . . .

and so do I.

**Color in the star next to each word you can read.**

| | | | |
|---|---|---|---|
| ☆ a | ☆ glad | ☆ mess | ☆ shall |
| ☆ all | ☆ happy | ☆ muddy | ☆ she |
| ☆ an | ☆ hat | ☆ nap | ☆ so |
| ☆ and | ☆ have | ☆ needs | ☆ stay |
| ☆ busy | ☆ help | ☆ nice | ☆ take |
| ☆ but | ☆ her | ☆ okay | ☆ tent |
| ☆ cat | ☆ I | ☆ out | ☆ the |
| ☆ comes | ☆ in | ☆ outside | ☆ then |
| ☆ Dad | ☆ inside | ☆ party | ☆ to |
| ☆ day | ☆ is | ☆ plan | ☆ upset |
| ☆ do | ☆ it | ☆ plays | ☆ wants |
| ☆ done | ☆ jumps | ☆ puddle | ☆ watch |
| ☆ dress-up | ☆ make | ☆ raining | ☆ we |
| ☆ dry | ☆ makes | ☆ saved | ☆ wear |
| ☆ feels | ☆ May | ☆ say | ☆ wet |
| ☆ for | ☆ me | ☆ says | ☆ yes |